AMY WU
and the
RIBBON
DANCE

For all the story time wiggle worms and dinnertime drummers! Keep dancing! —K. Z.

For Toru —C. C.

SIMON & SCHUSTER BOOKS FOR YOUNG READERS • An imprint of Simon & Schuster Children's Publishing Division • 1230 Avenue of the Americas, New York, New York 10020 • Text © 2023 by Kat Zhang • Illustration © 2023 by Charlene Chua • Book design by Laura Eckes © 2023 by Simon & Schuster, Inc. • All rights reserved, including the right of reproduction in whole or in part in any form. • SIMON & SCHUSTER BOOKS FOR YOUNG READERS and related marks are trademarks of Simon & Schuster, Inc. • For information about special discounts for bulk purchases, please contact Simon & Schuster Special Sales at 1-866-506-1949 or business@simonandschuster.com. • The Simon & Schuster Speakers Bureau can bring authors to your live event. For more information or to book an event, contact the Simon & Schuster Speakers Bureau at 1-866-248-3049 or visit our website at www.simonspeakers.com. • The text for this book was set in Andes Rounded. • The illustrations for this book were rendered digitally. • Manufactured in China • 0123 SCP • First Edition • 2 4 6 8 10 9 7 5 3 1 • CIP data for this book is available from the Library of Congress. • ISBN 978-1-6659-1672-1 • ISBN 978-1-6659-1673-8 (ebook)

AMY WU
and the
RIBBON DANCE

By **KAT ZHANG** Illustrated by **CHARLENE CHUA**

SIMON & SCHUSTER BOOKS FOR YOUNG READERS

New York   London   Toronto   Sydney   New Delhi

Amy Wu is **always** on the move.

During story time, she **wriggles** on the carpet.

During dinner, she **rap-tap-taps** chopsticks against her bowl.

"Stay still!" Mom says as Amy brushes her teeth . . .

or takes a bath . . .

or gets ready for bed.

But Amy cannot stay still.

She has to run—

jump—

skip—

twirl!

And today, Amy realizes one more thing she must do. . . .

Dance.

The women are fairies. Or butterflies. Or nymphs.
Their ribbons flutter and twist like they
have minds of their own.

Boom! Boom! go the drums.

Clack! Clack! go the bamboo clappers.

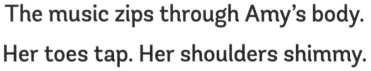

The music zips through Amy's body. Her toes tap. Her shoulders shimmy. This is dancing like she's never seen before. And it is **magic**.

Amy's mom smiles.

"Your friends are coming over this afternoon.

Do you want to have a dance party?"

"A **ribbon** dance party!"

shouts Amy.

Together, they call her classmates.

Willa will bring
her recorder.

Sam will bring
his drums.

And Lin will bring some
bamboo clappers.

But Amy is missing the most important
thing—**dancing ribbons.**

How can she make a dancing ribbon? Amy ties her hair ribbon to a chopstick with a big, strong knot. It's not **exactly** like the dancers' ribbons, but will it be close enough?

It's fun to shake the ribbon around, but it isn't the same. Her hair ribbon is too small and light. It flicks and snaps, but it doesn't flutter or twist.

Amy tries again. She ties her scarf to a knitting needle with a big, strong knot. It's not **exactly** like the dancers' ribbons, but will it be close enough?

It's fun to shake the scarf around,

but it isn't the same.

Her scarf is too
thick and heavy.

It wobbles and flops,
but it doesn't
flutter or twist.

Amy studies
her family's beautiful
lace tablecloth.

Hmm. . . .

"Oh, Amy," laughs Mom.

Mom dances with the tablecloth, but Amy doesn't join her.

She is too glum to skip. She is too sad to twirl.

A hair ribbon is not a dancing ribbon.

A scarf is not a dancing ribbon.

And a tablecloth is **definitely** not a dancing ribbon.

How will Amy and her friends dance without dancing ribbons?

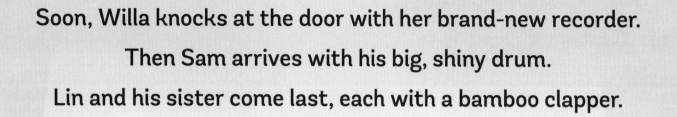

Soon, Willa knocks at the door with her brand-new recorder.

Then Sam arrives with his big, shiny drum.

Lin and his sister come last, each with a bamboo clapper.

They're all ready for the ribbon dance party.

But Amy is not.

"What's wrong?" asks Amy's dad.
"I think I know," says Amy's mom.

She waves Amy into her bedroom and takes a photo album from the shelf.

"Did you know I used to ribbon dance?"

Amy imagines her mom with fluttering, twisting ribbons.

Her shoulders slump lower.

Then Mom cracks open the album, and Amy's eyes grow wide.

There is her mom, surrounded by friends.

Dancing.

None of them has a dancing ribbon.

A melody drifts into the bedroom. It sounds like lute music.
It sounds like drums and bamboo clappers.

Boom! Boom!

Clack! Clack!

Amy follows the tune
into the hall.

There in the living room are Amy's friends.

"Where are your dancing ribbons?" asks Willa.

"Come join the fun!"

Amy hesitates.

A hair ribbon is not a dancing ribbon.

A scarf is not a dancing ribbon.

And a tablecloth is **definitely**
not a dancing ribbon.

But the music zips through her body.

Her toes **tap**. Her shoulders **shimmy**.

Her mom winks at her.

Amy smiles back.

Maybe the most important thing isn't dancing ribbons.

Maybe the most important thing is just to **dance**.

Amy hands Mom her hair ribbon. She gives Dad her scarf.

Grandma and Lin's little sister share the tablecloth.

Together, they skip around the coffee table and leap atop the couch.

They **run**—and **jump**—and **skip**—and **twirl**!

Amy dances with her friends, and her parents, and her grandma, too.

They are fairies. Or butterflies. Or nymphs.

And it is **magic**.

HOMEMADE DANCING RIBBONS

Ribbon dancing has a long, rich history in China. Dancers practice hard to perfect their skills and use ribbons that are many feet long to create beautiful patterns. Sometimes many dancers will perform together.

You don't need dancing ribbons to have an awesome dance party, but they certainly help! Luckily, many items you may already have in your home can be used to make your very own dancing ribbon.

IDEAS FOR THE RIBBON HANDLE:

1. A chopstick
2. A knitting needle
3. A drumstick
4. A stick

IDEAS FOR THE RIBBON:

1. A hair ribbon
2. A light scarf
3. A long sock
4. A strip of colored
   construction paper

Try mixing and matching the ideas above, or come up with some new ones of your own! You can attach the "ribbons" to the handles with a knot, like Amy, or with string or tape.

Now it's time for the dance party!
Put on some music and dance!